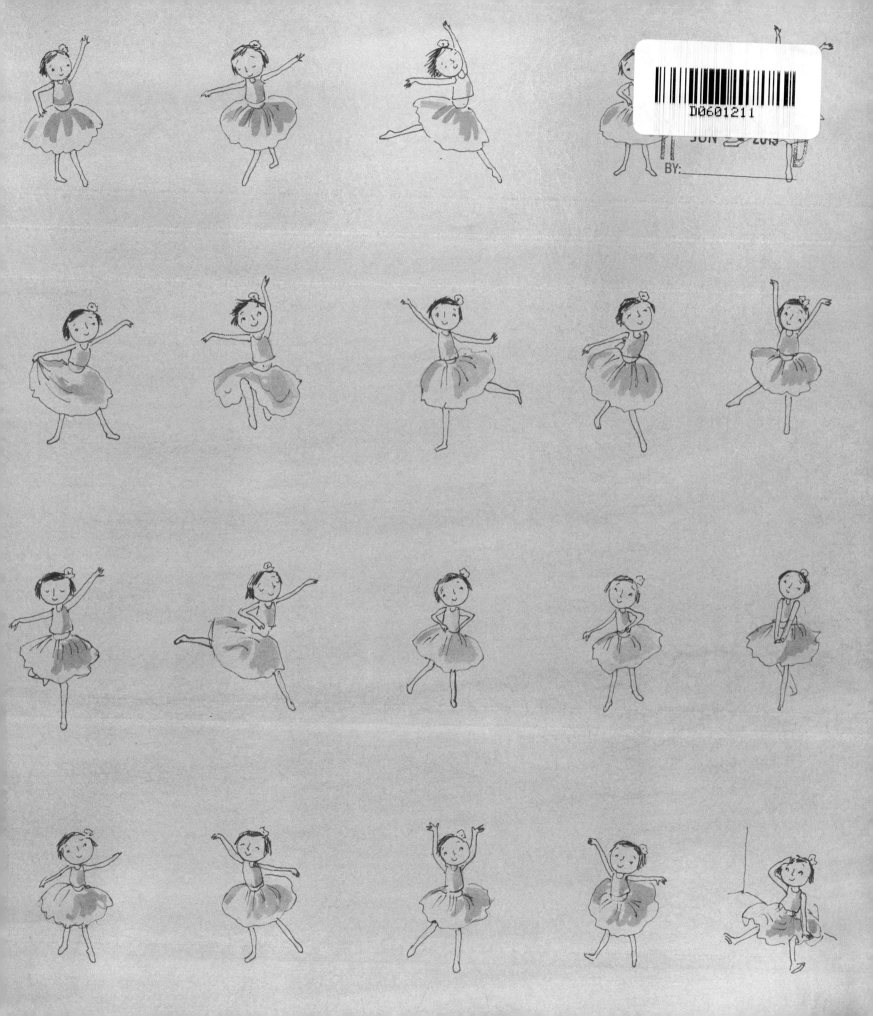

The school dance recital
was almost here!

Lena swirled

and twirled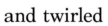

and jumped.

Lena's Slippers

Ioana Hobai

PAGE
STREET
KiDS

Lena's Slippers

Ioana Hobai

PAGE
STREET
KIDS

The school dance recital
was almost here!

Lena swirled

and twirled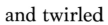

and jumped.

She did one last pirouette outside her classroom.
"Thank you! Thank you!" she whispered to her imaginary audience.

Taking a deep breath, she cracked the door open and tiptoed inside.
Mrs. Pascu did not tolerate tardiness.

As Lena slipped into her seat,
her teacher was already addressing the class.

"You'll all be daffodils in the recital this year," announced Mrs. Pascu.
"You need to have skirts or shorts in this color and you must have
white shirts and ballet slippers. Dress rehearsal will be next week."

"What if we can't find yellow fabric?" Lena whispered to Cristina.
At home, money was tight and the stores in town were half-empty.
Her parents had to wait in line for hours to buy anything—even milk.

Cristina shrugged.
Somehow, her parents could buy everything she needed.

After school, Lena rushed home
to try on last year's shirt and slippers.

The camisole was tight and a bit short
but it still fit her.

But the slippers . . .

"We'll have to buy new ones,"
her mom said, and sighed.

The next day Lena and her mother searched all over town for
yellow fabric. Finally, they found a shop with one roll left.

"It's not the right yellow!" protested Lena. "Mrs. Pascu is so picky!"

"Oh Lena," said her mom. "We're lucky to have found
any yellow at all. I'll sew you a beautiful skirt." It was getting late.
They still needed to find white slippers.

At the last store, they joined
a line of people waiting outside.

BALLET SLIPPERS
AVAILABLE
TODAY

Lena tried to be patient,
hoping for the best.

"Just five people ahead of us,"
she counted.

"Look, there's Marcella!"

"SOLD OUT!"
shouted the sales lady.

Lena watched as Marcella
left with the last pair of
white slippers.

That night, Lena tossed and turned.
Cristina would certainly have a perfect skirt,
Lydia's slippers still fit, and Marcella . . .
oh, how unfair!

On the day of dress rehearsal, Lena tried to hide,
but Mrs. Pascu spotted her right away.

"Lena, that skirt isn't the right yellow!
And where are your slippers?"
Lena felt her chest tighten.

"You cannot dance in socks,"
snapped Mrs. Pascu. "You must
have white slippers!"

When Lena arrived home,
she needed some cheering up.

Luckily, her father had
a surprise.

"A friend from work gave me
his daughter's old slippers for you,"
he said. "I hope they fit."

"Thank you, Daddy!" she cried,
tearing open the newspaper wrapping.

"Oh. They're not the color
Mrs. Pascu asked for."

"No one will care," said her dad.
"Your dancing is what matters." Lena nodded. But she knew
how much it mattered to Mrs. Pascu.

The recital was only a couple of days away. Lena tried to squish her toes into her old white slippers one more time.

They still didn't fit.

Perhaps if she cut them in pieces and glued them on the brown ones?

Or colored the brown slippers
with white chalk?

Or a white crayon?

Nothing worked.

At school, everyone was excited
about the upcoming recital.

The night before the performance, Lena couldn't eat her dinner.
She had dreamed about dancing for so long. What if
Mrs. Pascu wouldn't let her dance at all?

Suddenly, she had an idea. It could work . . .

The big day arrived. Lena tiptoed backstage
in her newly-white slippers, past Mrs. Pascu,
her heartbeat drumming in her temples.

The curtains parted. The lights were blinding.
The music started.

Lena's heart swelled with the music. This was the moment
she had waited for all year. She swirled and twirled
and jumped, forgetting all her worries.

She did one last pirouette, took a giant leap, and . . .

landed to thunderous applause.

She bowed gracefully, whispering
"Thank you! Thank you!"

Lena closed her eyes for a brief moment to take it all in and
then dashed to join her parents in the audience.

She turned her gaze towards the stage and smiled.
She could already picture her next dance.

This story was inspired by a memory from my childhood. I grew up in Romania during the '70s and '80s, in a time of economic hardship, harsh rules, and strict teachers.

Sometimes the schools organized makeshift dance performances, usually with a patriotic theme. These recitals were a burden on most families because the dance costumes were handmade and materials, such as fabric, were limited. People were creative by necessity and could improvise costumes with very few supplies.

I was terrified of my teacher, the real Mrs. Pascu, because she always demanded things that were hard to find. Back then, saying no to any authority figure was not an option. For one particular performance I needed white slippers, but the only ones I had were a pair of brown hand-me-downs from my sister.

I came up with the same solution as Lena: I painted the slippers white the night before, dried them on the radiator, and performed . . . making a total mess on the stage. But unlike Lena, my true passion as a child was drawing. It was something I did all the time, from morning till night, with the same love that Lena has for dancing. It provided an escape to a world without worries, where I could set my own rules.

For my parents.

Copyright © 2019 Ioana Hobai. First published in 2019 by Page Street Kids, an imprint of Page Street Publishing Co. 27 Congress Street, Suite 105, Salem, MA 01970 www.pagestreetpublishing.com. All rights reserved. No part of this book may be reproduced or used, in any form or by any means, electronic or mechanical, without prior permission in writing from the publisher. Distributed by Macmillan, sales in Canada by The Canadian Manda Group. ISBN-13: 978-1-62414-695-4 ISBN-10: 1-62414-695-3. CIP data for this book is available from the Library of Congress. This book was typeset in Marion. The illustrations were done in ink, watercolor, and acrylic. Printed and bound in China. 19 20 21 22 23 xxx 5 4 3 2 1

Page Street Publishing uses only materials from suppliers who are committed to responsible and sustainable forest management. Page Street Publishing protects our planet by donating to nonprofits like The Trustees, which focuses on local land conservation.